A Gift For

MADELINE LEE

From

SANTA ♡

How to Use Your Interactive Story Buddy®:

1. Move the switch in the battery compartment to "On."
2. Activate your Story Buddy by pressing the "On / Off" button on the ear.
3. Read the story aloud in a quiet place. Speak in a clear voice when you see the highlighted phrases.
4. Listen to your Story Buddy respond with several different phrases throughout the book.

Clarity and speed of reading affect the way Rudolph® responds. He may not always respond to young children.

Watch for even more Interactive Story Buddy characters. For more information, visit us on the Web at Hallmark.com/StoryBuddy.

Hallmark's **I Reply Technology** brings your Story Buddy to life! When you read the key phrases out loud, your Story Buddy gives a variety of responses, so each time you read feels as magical as the first.

Rudolph the Red-Nosed Reindeer © & ® or ™ The Rudolph Co., L.P. All elements under license to Character Arts, LLC. All rights reserved.

Published by Hallmark Gift Books, a division of Hallmark Cards, Inc., Kansas City, MO 64141 Visit us on the Web at Hallmark.com.

Editorial Director: Delia Berrigan
Editor: Emily Osborn
Art Director: Chris Opheim
Designer: Mary Eakin
Production Designer: Bryan Ring

ISBN: 978-1-59530-677-7
1XKT2403

Printed and bound in China
JUN14

BOOK 2

RUDOLPH®

AND THE
SOUTH POLE TOYS

By Chelsea Resnick | Illustrated by Ed Myer

Hallmark

In Christmas Town, the world's most magical place, there lived the world's most famous reindeer, Rudolph, whose nose was red as a Christmas berry. It even glowed!

Rudolph was a clever, kind, and helpful reindeer who loved spending Christmastime with his friends and family. He didn't look like all the other reindeer, but that was fine with him. He didn't mind being different.

It was one year after Rudolph saved Christmas, and tomorrow was Christmas Eve. Rudolph got a letter from his old friend, King Moonracer. The king ruled over the Island of Misfit Toys, a place where the world's forgotten and unwanted toys went to live.

Dear Rudolph,

I need your help!
Please come to the
Island of Misfit Toys.

Urgently,
King Moonracer

Rudolph quickly flew to the island.

"Rudolph! You're here!" said the king. "A toy airplane tried to bring three toys back to the island, but its compass was upside-down. Now the toys are stuck in the South Pole instead of the North Pole.

There's a flying dollhouse, a purring T-Rex, and a bubble-blowing harmonica. I'm running out of time to fetch them before Christmas. Could you please go to the South Pole and bring them back?"

"Why, of course!" said Rudolph. He knew he had to help.

Rudolph asked his best friends, Hermey, Cornelius, and Bumble, to come along.

Rudolph hitched up a sleigh and set off for the South Pole.

When the stranded toys saw Rudolph's shiny red nose, they cheered.

"It's Rudolph the Red-Nosed Reindeer!" said the dollhouse.

"We're saved!" said the T-Rex.

With bubbles fizzing everywhere, the harmonica cried,
"I love you, Rudolph!"

Rudolph and his friends hopped out of the sleigh.
Cornelius told the Bumble to wait there.

Rudolph was thrilled they'd found the toys. But—drat
and double-drat!—they couldn't get inside the igloo. The
window and door were encrusted with ice. Rudolph tugged with
all his might. Cornelius and Hermey tried, too. But no luck!

"Don't worry!" Rudolph shouted to the toys. "We'll get you out!"

Cornelius went to fetch ice picks. Maybe they could chip the ice off the door.

Rudolph was so thankful he found friends like these.

Rudolph stood in front of the igloo. Suddenly the ground shook. BOOM! BOOM! BOOM!

The Bumble was marching toward the igloo! He threw back his head and roared.

"Uh-oh!" said Rudolph. "The Bumble looks upset! Cornelius, come quickly!"

The toys were trapped. The Bumble was acting crazed. Rudolph shook his head.

This was a huge disaster!

The Bumble got closer and closer. Rudolph didn't know what to do.

"Cornelius!" he shouted again.

But before Cornelius got there, the Bumble walked over to the igloo. Then he lifted it clean off the ground! The toys were saved!

"Yippee skippy!" cried the toys. "We're free!"

The Bumble had just wanted to help. Rudolph was utterly dumbfounded.

When Rudolph and his friends landed at the workshop, Santa was there to greet the new toys. "Well, hello! I know three little children who will love finding you on Christmas morning."

The toys bounced up and down.

"Homes for Christmas!" said the T-Rex.

"My dreams! They're coming true!" cried the dollhouse.

"I feel SO holly jolly!" bubbled the harmonica.

Rudolph smiled. He loved working for the magical man himself, Santa Claus.

Christmas Eve arrived. Santa and the reindeer worked hard until the break of dawn. Afterward, Rudolph was tired. But it was fun helping so many toys find homes for Christmas.

Now it was time to go home and spend Christmas with the ones he loved. His family was the greatest. And he was so thankful he found friends like these.

Hermey and Cornelius nibbled fruitcake. The reindeer munched on spiced apples.

They sang songs and opened presents. Rudolph was having an amazing Christmas!

Finally, Rudolph caught the Bumble's eye. He was glad the snow monster had been at the South Pole to help.

"Merry Christmas, you bighearted Bumble!" said Rudolph.

The Bumble smiled and roared—which was his way of saying, "Merry Christmas, Rudolph!"

Did you have fun reading with Rudolph®?
We would love to hear from you!

Please send your comments to:
Hallmark Book Feedback
P.O. Box 419034
Mail Drop 100
Kansas City, MO 64141

Or e-mail us at: booknotes@hallmark.com